IZZY Itzhak's Instrument Invention

Kirsten B. King
Pictures by Mary G. Olson

Childpress CB Books

Dedicated to my four (now grown) children: Kenny, Danny, Greta and Tim. Thanks for imagining and inventing with me all these years! I love you!
—KBK

Dedicated to my amazingly creative adult children Carl, Mark, Sara and especially Dan who brought this book, conceived so long ago, to publication.
—MGO

In Indianapolis, Indiana
        it was easy to find
an interesting gentleman
        who was clever and kind.

"Izzy Itzhak Instrument Maker"
was hung over the door
of his instrument workshop
(that was also a store).

Izzy made instruments
of all different types;
bells and bassoons
and organs with pipes.
It never mattered to Izzy
how long it would take
to make some that would whistle
and some that should shake.

Nothing brought Izzy
more joy and delight,
than working all day
and into the night.
He'd carve and he'd polish
and tighten up springs
and when he was finished
he'd tune up the strings.

One day a musician walked into the town,
an important musician who was known all around.

"Excuse me, Mr. Itzhak" he said with great flair,
"I'd love to see all that you're working on there.
I'm impressed with your work; I enjoy it immensely.
Make something for me!" he insisted intensely.

"Come back here on Monday, I'll have something for you."
said the instrument maker, as he thought it through.

Then Izzy got busy.

On Monday, Izzy Itzhak made a new mandolin.
But the musician just sighed, and to Izzy's chagrin
he said, "That's not the instrument I imagined I'd see.
Can you please get busy on a new one for me?"

On Tuesday, Izzy Itzhak
    made a new tambourine.
The musician exclaimed,
    "That's the nicest I've seen!"
But then added, "It's still not
    what I imagined I'd see.
Can you please get busy
    on a new one for me?"

On Wednesday, Izzy's whistle
was made with a slide.

The musician apologized,
    "Deep down inside,
    it's still not the instrument
    I imagined I'd see.

I'm sorry, but please make
    a new one for me."

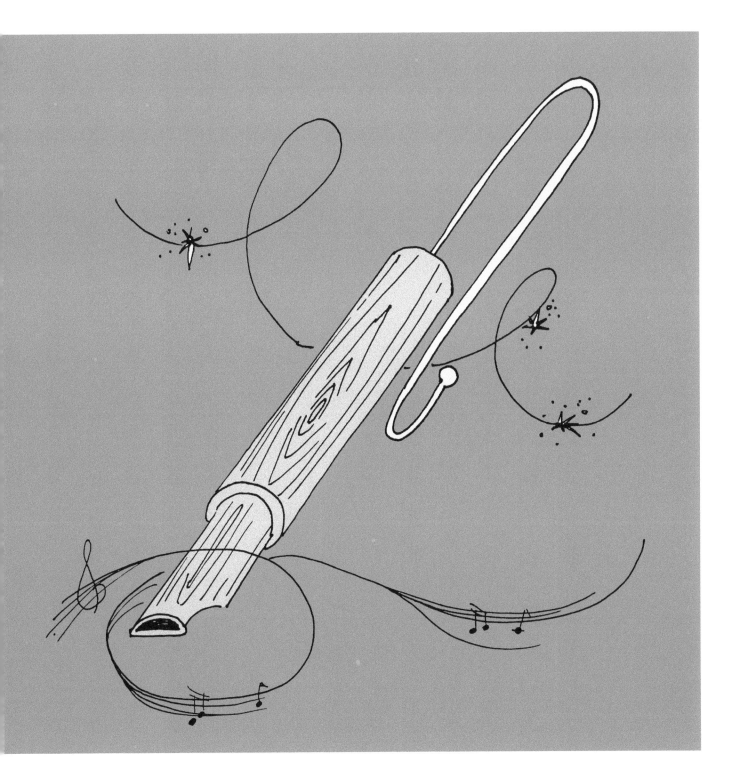

On Thursday, Izzy's tuba made a thunderous noise;
the kind that would please all the girls and the boys.
But the musician just said, "I don't like what I see.
Can you please get busy on a new one for me?"

On Friday, Izzy crafted a fine, fancy, flute.
But as soon as the musician heard it *toot-toot* ...

he said, "It is fancy,
but I don't like what I see.
Please try one more time
to make something for me."

On Saturday, Izzy worked
with new instrument plans.

He intended to use some
combs and some cans.
Izzy gathered up strings
and cartons and glue,
scissors and buttons and
bells and tape too.

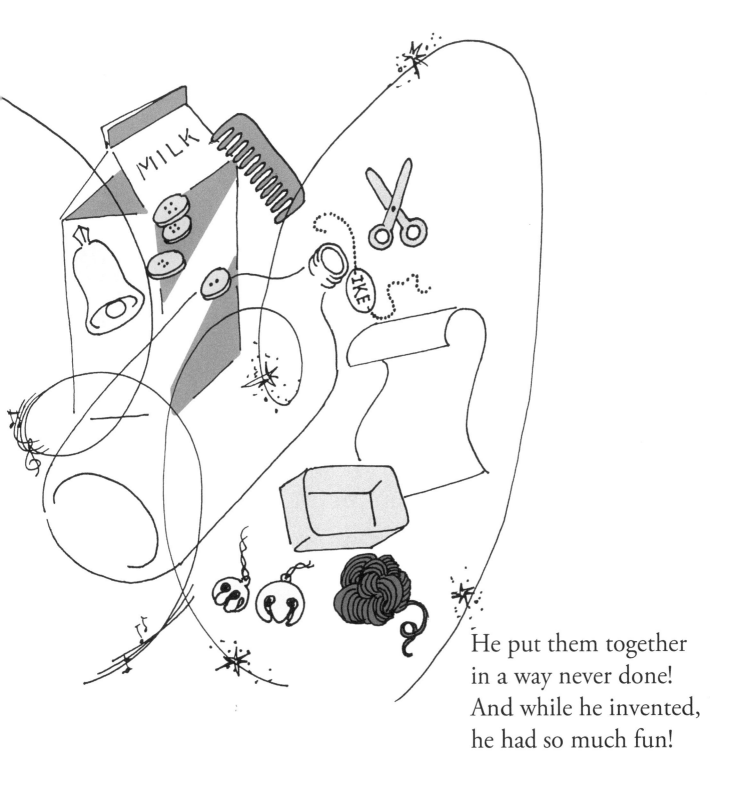

He put them together
in a way never done!
And while he invented,
he had so much fun!

When the musician returned,
    he stood up and said,
"Thanks, Izzy, for this instrument
    that came from your head!
I never saw one before,
    but you imagined it well!
I'm happy and pleased
    and so glad! Can you tell?"

Izzy sat and he smiled;
    he had made up his mind.
He would no longer make instruments
    of the usual kind.
"Each instrument I make will
    be an imaginative invention!"
And to let everyone know
    of his brand-new intention—

He remade his sign where the people would enter.
He took off the "Maker" and put up "Inventor."

Note to the reader:
You might be thinking you wish you had seen,
The instrument imagined on Saturday's scene.
But can I encourage you to make one yourself
with stuff that you find up on your own shelf?
Your imagination is fabulous; you can make one as well!
And it will be great! I can already tell.

Izzy Itzhak

The End

CPSIA information can be obtained
at www.ICGtesting.com
Printed in the USA
LVHW070705010522
717643LV00005B/19